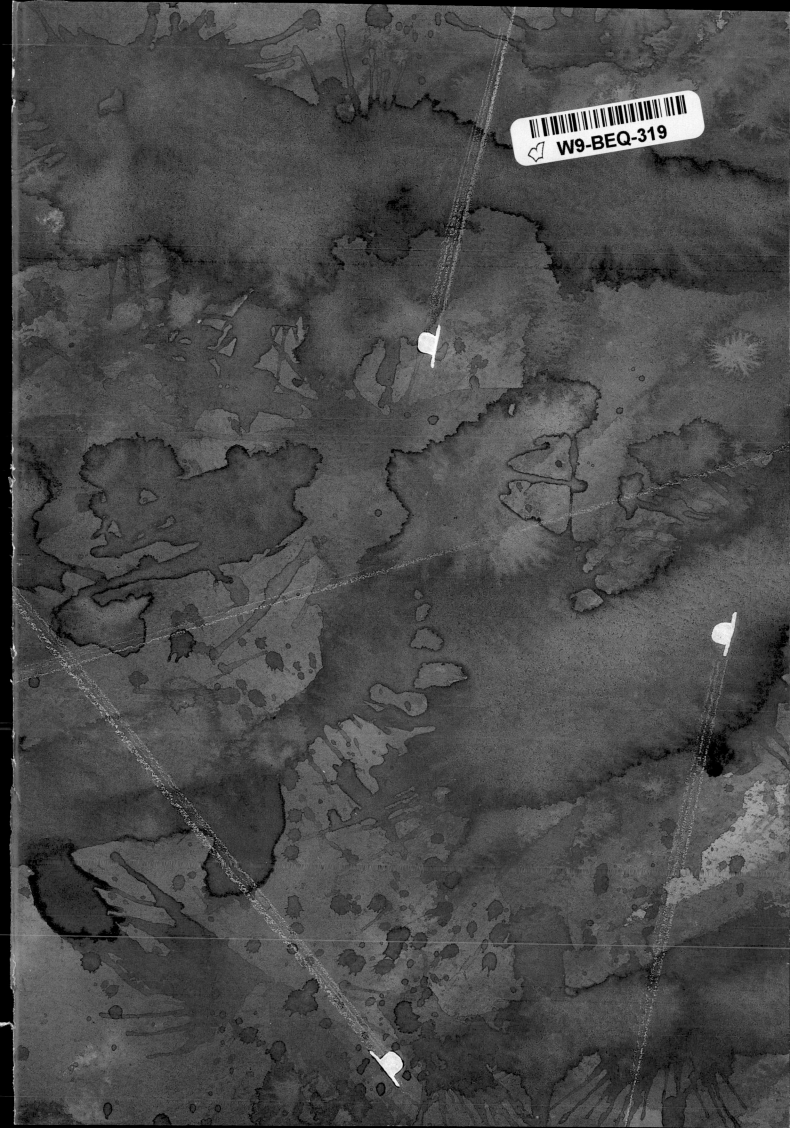

Eric Sauté

Rabén & Sjögren Stockholm

Translation copyright © 1988 by Angela Barnett-Lindberg
All rights reserved
Originally published in Sweden by Rabén & Sjögren under the title *Hattjakten,*
text and illustrations copyright © 1987 by Sven Nordqvist
Library of Congress catalog card number: 88-4710
Printed in Italy, 1988
First edition, 1988

R&S Books are distributed in the United States of America by Farrar, Straus and Giroux, New York;
in the United Kingdom by Ragged Bears, Andover;
and in Australia by ERA Publications, Adelaide

ISBN 91 29 59070 1

The Hat Hunt

Sven Nordqvist

Translated by Angela Barnett-Lindberg

R&S
BOOKS

Stockholm   New York   Toronto   London   Adelaide

Grandpa has a hat which he never takes off – except
when he goes to bed. The last thing he does every evening is
hang it over his bedside lamp. And the first thing he does
every morning is put it on.

But one morning when Grandpa wakes up, his hat is
gone! When he has turned over everything that can be
turned over at least three times, and has patted his head at
least seven times, he stomps into the kitchen, mad as a
hornet.

"Someone has taken my hat!" he shouts. "Is this your idea of a joke?"

Grandpa's dog, Lightning, has been sleeping on the kitchen table. He opens one eye and says: "I never make jokes before dinner. You should know that. I've been lying here resting since dinner yesterday, and I intend to go on resting until it's time for dinner today."

"Oh, yes, you're a fine guard dog," scolds Grandpa. "There's been a robbery here. Thieves and gangsters have stolen my hat!"

"I've told you a thousand times, I'm not a guard dog," says Lightning. "I'm a pet dog. Now drink your coffee and calm down."

"Coffee," says Grandpa grumpily. "How can I possibly drink coffee without a hat on my head. And *what* is this?"

Grandpa fishes a tin soldier out of the coffee jar. He drinks three cups of coffee while he wonders how the tin soldier could have gotten into the jar.

"By the way," mutters Lightning. "I dreamed your old hat flew over to Mrs. Hen's house."

"Why didn't you tell me that right away?" grumbles Grandpa. He puts the tin soldier in his breast pocket and runs off.

Mrs. Hen is in her garden, knitting.

"Good morning, Mrs. Hen," says Grandpa. "I am looking for my hat. Thieves stole it in the night while I was sleeping tight. Have you seen anything?"

"In the night, while you were sleeping tight?" says Mrs. Hen. "Night, tight, fright, sight. I can't understand what you're talking about. I'm knitting. I can't hear anything, and I can't see anything. I just sit where I sit. There's coffee in the fridge, wafers in the pot. Do help yourself, pour and dunk, but don't talk. I'll take care of that."

While Mrs. Hen talks, Grandpa helps himself to a cup of coffee and a wafer. When he bites into the wafer's chocolate filling, he finds a piece of a watch chain.

He is just about to ask Mrs. Hen why it is there when she says: "Talk to Someone in the old barn about the night when you were sleeping tight. Someone knows more than you think. Someone is probably keeping track of hats."

Grandpa puts the watch chain in his pocket and goes directly to the old barn.

It is quite light inside. Tall prune palms, chrysanthemums, strawberry trees, and sugarcane grow under a large hole in the roof.

No one is visible in this greenery. But Someone is there. Someone who doesn't want to be seen, not even by Grandpa.

Someone lives in a crate in the middle of all the plants.

A note hangs on the crate: "Hello, Grandpa. I had to go out for a while. But do have some coffee and cake. You know where to find it."

Grandpa snorts. It is always the same. Someone is never home when he comes to visit. He finds a cup and fills it with coffee from the tap.

"Has Someone seen my hat?" he calls out into the silence. Then he waits.

After a while, a little toy car arrives. The note in it says: "P.S. Your hat went past here before. It disappeared in the junk pile."

Grandpa begins to search through the junk pile.

"Someone should clean up here," he shouts. "Vacuum!"

He can't see the hat anywhere. Instead, he finds a small pen-knife. He inspects it carefully. It looks very familiar, but Grandpa's memory will not stretch quite that far.

The little car comes whizzing back. It goes across the junk pile and disappears under an old sheet hanging from the top of the wall. Grandpa follows it.

He walks right into Tailor Button-Up's shop. The tailor is lying face down across a large table, cutting some material.

"Hello, Button-Up. Is the shop open on Sundays?"

"Oh, what? Open? One minute, I'll check," says the tailor. He goes over to the front door and tries to open it.

"No, sorry, we're closed. You'll have to come again on Friday."

"I'm looking for my hat," says Grandpa. "I think it may have disappeared in here. But don't you recognize me?"

Tailor Button-Up bends over nearly double and squints at Grandpa. It is not until he puts a hat on Grandpa's head that he recognizes him.

"Oh, now I see, it's Grandpa. I've never seen you without a hat before."

He pulls at Grandpa's nightshirt. "Have you been trying on a new shirt? How nice! It suits you. It costs ten dollars, but you can have it for only two."

"Have you seen my hat?" asks Grandpa, trying to control himself.

"Yes," says Button-Up happily. "It's very beautiful. I have never seen *precisely* such a hat look so elegant before. But why aren't you wearing it?"

"Because it has disappeared!" shouts Grandpa.

"Please don't shout, my good man; I'm not blind. Perhaps you would like some coffee?"

"Yes, please." Grandpa sighs and sits down heavily.

Tailor Button-Up hands Grandpa a plate and a thermos.

"Help yourself. Believe me, I've got other things to do," he says, and goes to stand by the door.

When Grandpa pours the coffee, a little magnet tumbles out of the thermos. He picks it up. He is quite sure that he owned one like it a long time ago.

"There was a magnet in the coffee," he says.

"Ugh. Maggots are such unpleasant insects. Throw it away so you don't burn your tongue," says the tailor. "Hmmm, that's very strange," he continues thoughtfully. "The hat which you are not wearing is out there, flying. Why? Does it usually do that?"

Grandpa leaps up. "What did you say? Where is it?"

"It disappeared down there behind the fence," says Button-Up. "Just think how clever they are nowadays. They even fly!"

Grandpa races to the fence. Then he stops, panting.

"Come and buy thousands of things, lovely, lovely things. Not very expensive, just very cheap," a voice shouts right into his ear, making him jump.

There stands a rabbit selling little objects from a stall.

"My goodness, how you startled me," says Grandpa.

"No danger, don't worry. Rabbity doesn't bite much."

"Have you seen my hat fly by?" asks Grandpa.

"No hats today, sorry," says Rabbity. "Tomorrow we shall have lovely new ones. But we have lots of other things. Please come and look, look, look!"

There are key rings and odd socks and bread crumblers and erasers and fish-hooks and back scratchers and old football tickets and trembling rubber skeletons.

"A dollar each. One hundred fifty for the lot. Best quality. Real plastic and metal."

"That's a lot of junk you've got there," says Grandpa. "Do you have any motorcycles?"

"One moment, I'll look in the stockroom," says Rabbity, and disappears through a loose board in the fence.

While he is gone, Grandpa looks in a box marked "Free." He finds an old whistle. It probably doesn't work, but Grandpa likes it anyway and puts it in his pocket.

Rabbity pokes his head out through the fence.

"Come and look, my old customer."

There, on the other side, stands a broken-down, rusty motorcycle with a sidecar.

"It's a Bugatti," says Rabbity. "As good as new. Costs only ten, eleven dollars. Very good. Just needs a bit of oil, and it'll work wonderfully."

"I'll believe that when I see it," says Grandpa, and sits down in the sidecar. "We'll take it on a test run first and see if we can catch up with my hat."

"No problem," says Rabbity. "I'll just tank it up."

He pours in half a bottle of cherry soda. Then he turns everything that can be turned and tries to start it. The motorcycle doesn't budge.

"I can fix it," says Grandpa. "If there's one thing I know about, it's motorcycles. Just give me a wrench and a hammer, and I'll take care of it."

Now he is in a fine mood. He fiddles and hammers and squirts oil, until the rabbit is terribly impressed.

"Let's try again. Helmet on, Rabbit, because here we go!"

Off it goes! They jump over the fence and skid onto a narrow road.

Just like the good old days, thinks Grandpa.

"You're a real old-timer, my good customer," shouts Rabbity and kisses Grandpa right on the mouth.

"This is fantabulous. I'll raise the price to fourteen bucks. Shall I put her in second gear?"

"By golly, yes, just keep going," yells Grandpa. "Might as well put her in fourth right away."

He should never have said that.
Vrooom, the motorcycle shoots off like a
comet. They race over one field, and
another, and then comes a meadow, and
then comes a stone! Bang, the motorcycle
goes up into the air, and out falls Grandpa.
He does a backward somersault and lands
on the grass. He hears the rattling and
sputtering of the motorcycle as it disappears into the hills, and soon everything
is still.

In fact, it becomes quite silent. Grandpa thinks he can hear the warm air rising from the ground. Fields and woods bask in the sparkling summer light.

Grandpa feels tired. I'll never see my old hat again, he thinks. But what does it matter, anyway? Then he remembers the five small objects he found on his hat hunt.

From his breast pocket, Grandpa takes out the tin soldier, the watch chain, the penknife, the magnet, and the whistle. He sets them on a stone.

Now he remembers. He had absolutely just precisely these five objects in his pocket a long, long time ago.

He was just seven years old when his friend Adam showed him a hedgehog that he kept in a box. Little Grandpa wanted it very badly.

"Can I buy it?" Grandpa asked.

"What have you got?" said Adam.

Grandpa lined up the tin soldier, the piece of watch chain, the penknife, the magnet, and the whistle. It was quiet for a long time. This moment is bright and clear in Grandpa's memory: the five objects, the box with the hedgehog, Adam's hand letting go of the box and picking up the tin soldier, the silence.

It was a difficult moment for little Grandpa. If Adam said yes, he would have to give up his five dearest possessions. But in return he would get a hedgehog, which he could give milk to every day.

"That'll do. Now let's trade, and the trade is forever."

Grandpa took the box and ran home. He was so happy that his heart jumped for joy.

Grandpa doesn't remember everything that clearly. But he remembers that his mother said you couldn't keep a hedgehog in a box. It would die.

Grandpa set his hedgehog free in Great-grandma's garden and gave it milk as soon as it came out, so it would know where its home was. Grandpa remembers that he stroked its quills. It did not feel especially nice, but what can you do if you love someone?

There Grandpa sits in the large summer meadow and remembers what it was like to be seven years old and have a hedgehog and a great-grandma and a mother and father and five brothers and sisters. He has gotten all these memories back just because his hat ran away. Grandpa has seen a lot in his time, but he doesn't understand how this could happen.

Grandpa goes home. He doesn't care about the hat any-more. He places the five small objects on the desk in the living room. Then he looks for another hat in the closet.

Perhaps I can wear this one, he thinks. No, I don't think so. I don't have to wear a hat just because I'm an old man. There's still a lot of summer left.

It will be time for a hat soon enough.

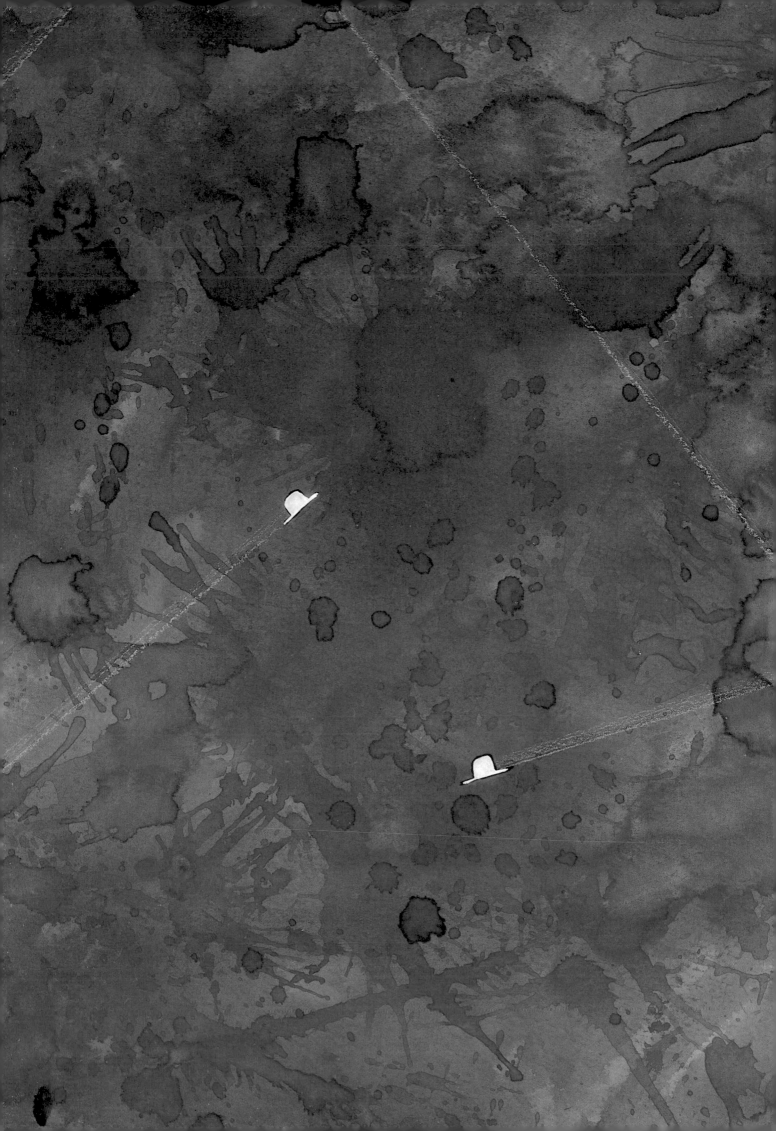